I AM READING

Jumping Jack

A. H. BENJAMIN

ILLUSTRATED BY

GARRY PARSONS

KINGFISHER
NEW YORK

For Flynn—A. H. B
To Oliver and Edward—G. P.

Text copyright © 2009 by A. H. Benjamin
Illustrations copyright © 2009 by Garry Parsons
Published in the United States by Kingfisher,
175 Fifth Ave., New York, NY 10010
Kingfisher is an imprint of Macmillan Children's Books, London.

Distributed in the U.S. by Macmillan, 175 Fifth Ave., New York, NY 10010
Distributed in Canada by H.B. Fenn and Company Ltd., 34 Nixon Road, Bolton, Ontario L7E 1W2

Library of Congress Cataloging-in-Publication data has been applied for.

ISBN: 978-0-7534-6297-3

Kingfisher books are available for special promotions and premiums. For details contact: Special Markets
Department, Macmillan, 175 Fifth Avenue, New York, NY 10010.

For more information, please visit www.kingfisherpublications.com

First American Edition November 2009
Printed in China
10 9 8 7 6 5 4 3 2 1

Contents

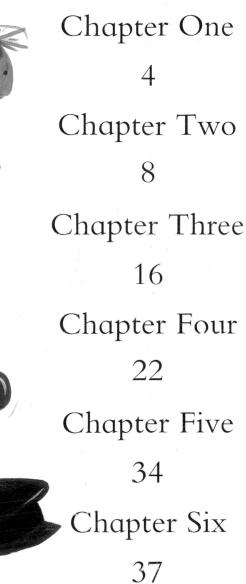

Chapter One

Jack was watching the Olympics on television.

His favorite event was the high jump.

I wish I could jump that high! thought Jack, goggle-eyed.

Just then his uncle walked into the
room. He was in the navy. He always
brought Jack unusual presents.
"Look what I've got
for you!" he said,
shaking a jar.

"What is it?" Jack said with a frown.

"Jumping beans!" his uncle said, smiling.
"They are from South America!"

"Do they really jump?" asked Jack.

"Of course they do," replied his uncle.
To show Jack, he put a few beans on
the coffee table.

They started jumping like crazy.

Click! Click! Click! They jumped all
over the place.
One hit the TV screen.
Another struck the
ceiling, bounced back
down, and hit the
cat's nose.

Jack laughed with
delight.
He could hardly
believe his eyes.
"Wow, they do jump!" he cried
excitedly. "They're going to be fun!"
And they were . . .

7

Chapter Two

Then one day Grandma came to visit. She knew nothing about the jumping beans. So when she found them in the kitchen one morning, she cooked them for Jack's breakfast.

Jack was in a hurry to go to school that day. He did not realize what they were until he had gobbled them all up!

"But they weren't for eating!" he whined, very upset. "Just for playing with!"
"You shouldn't play with your food," Grandma told him sternly.

Jack's troubles began as soon as he stepped out the front door. One moment he was walking down the step . . .

. . . and the next
he was flying over
the fence . . .

. . . Thud! He landed on the sidewalk.

How did I do that? wondered Jack, amazed. *I didn't mean to jump!* Thinking no more about it, he continued on his way to school. Then, all of a

sudden . . . Whoosh! He jumped so
high that he hit his head on a branch.

"I've done it again!" cried Jack as he
lay sprawled on the ground. "What on
earth is happening to me?"
Then he remembered: the jumping beans!

"Oh no!" he gasped. "They're making me jump!"

Very worried, he staggered to his feet. Jack had not gone far when he jumped yet again. This time he found himself sitting on a police officers's shoulders.

"What are you doing?" demanded the police officer sternly. "Get off now!"

"Er, sorry, sir," stammered Jack. "I . . . It's the jumping beans, you see."

But the police officer just gave him an angry stare, and Jack quickly hurried off.

Chapter Three

Jack soon came to a busy street. While waiting to cross, he noticed an old woman standing beside him.

"I'll help you cross," offered Jack kindly.

"Oh, thank you," the old woman said
with a smile as Jack took her hand.
No sooner had he done so than both
he and the woman left the ground.
Right over the busy traffic they flew,
landing on the other side of the street.

"That was a dangerous thing to do!"
croaked the old woman, very shaken.
"Who do you think you are?
Superman?"

Poor Jack had to run all the way to
school. Luckily he arrived there
without any more troubles.

In class he sat stiffly on his chair,
praying he would not jump again.

But he did . . .

Crash! He landed on the teacher's desk.

The class laughed.

But the teacher was not amused.

"Go stand in the corner!" she ordered.

Red-faced, Jack obeyed.

In the corner where he stood was a long pipe running from the floor to the ceiling. He held on to it tightly with both arms. Just in case.

But then he began to jump.
He could not keep his feet
on the floor, no matter
how hard he tried.

Up and
down, up
and down
he slid
along the pipe.
He looked like a
wind-up toy.
This time even the teacher
laughed along with the class.

Chapter Four

In the playground, things got even
worse for Jack. Now he jumped
nonstop. Boing! Boing! Boing! he
went, as if he had springs on his feet.

"Look at Jack! Look at Jack!" cried the children, shrieking and laughing excitedly. "Look at how he's jumping!" A teacher and a lunch lady saw him, and they went to help. They each grabbed Jack by a leg and tried to keep him down.

"Stop jumping!" they shouted.

"I can't help it!" Jack shouted back.

For quite a while all three of them bounced up and down. The other children thought that was hilarious. They laughed even more.

In the end the teacher and the lunch lady had to let go of Jack.

"He's completely out of control!" they said, panting.

It was true, because Jack was now jumping quicker and higher. He even bounced on the school roof, where the custodian was doing some repairs.

Jack almost scared the life out of him.
I'm going to end up on the moon! thought
poor Jack.

Now there was complete chaos in the playground. Everyone tried to get out of Jack's way. They didn't want to be squashed!

"Everyone inside!" shouted the principal. "That boy is getting too dangerous!" And they all rushed inside the school.

The principal had had enough.

He decided to call the police. They
came right away, with their loud sirens.

But they could not catch Jack. Even
with their speedy cars.
"No way!" they said.

Then the school called the fire department. They soon arrived in their bright red fire engines.

But they could not catch Jack either.

Even with their tall ladders.

"No chance!" they said.

After that the school called the army.
They showed up within minutes, with
their tanks rolling and helicopters
whizzing.

But they could not catch Jack. Even
with their special nets.
"Impossible!" they said.
They all gave up.

Chapter Five

Then Grandma strode into the
playground, angrily waving her cane
in the air.

"Leave my Jack alone!" she ordered.
"He's done nothing wrong. He's just
full of beans!"

Grandma told them to listen. She explained what she had done. "But I haven't cooked them all," she added, pulling a handful of beans from her coat pocket. "See?"

And before anyone could say *Jumping Jack*, she swallowed them all. "Sorry," she said, grinning, "but it's the only way to catch Jack."

Chapter Six

The jumping beans worked instantly—
because they were not cooked. All of a
sudden . . . zoom! Grandma shot up
into the sky like a rocket. She caught
Jack right away!

Everyone cheered and clapped.

Then, hand in hand, Jack and Grandma bounced out of the playground to more cheers and clapping.

"Where are we going?" cried Jack, tired of jumping.

"Anywhere we like," said Grandma, smiling. She had wanted to stop Jack jumping, but now she was enjoying herself. "This is fun!"

They kept on bouncing.

They went over tall buildings . . .

. . . churches, rivers, and bridges . . .

. . . parks and soccer fields . . .

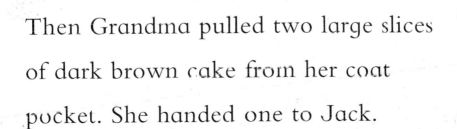

Then Grandma pulled two large slices
of dark brown cake from her coat
pocket. She handed one to Jack.

"What is it?" asked Jack.

"It's called chocolate concrete," explained Grandma. "I made it very quickly when I heard that you were in trouble. It gets so heavy in your stomach when you eat it that it will stop you from jumping. And me, too!"

Jack gobbled up his chocolate concrete. "Mmm, not bad at all!" said Grandma, busy munching on her own slice.

"Anyway, it should start working soon."

And it did . . . They started bouncing lower and lower . . . until they stopped completely.

Back home, Jack slumped on the sofa. He was exhausted but also very relieved.

"I will never, ever jump again!" he said. "Never, ever!"

"Oh, you never know," Grandma told him.

"Never, ever!" said Jack again.

But he was wrong. When he got older, he became an Olympic champion in the high jump. Jumping Jack won lots of gold medals!

About the author and illustrator

A. H. Benjamin is a successful children's author with more than 20 books to his name. "I got the idea for *Jumping Jack* when I learned that jumping beans really jump," Attia says, "but I would not like to be Jack because I am scared of heights!"

Garry Parsons is an award-winning illustrator of many children's books. He also does artwork for magazines and advertisements. He likes drawing, painting, and eating baked beans. "I really like being an illustrator," Garry says, "but I would have loved to have been an Olympic athlete like Jack."

Strategies for Independent Readers

Predict

Think about the cover, illustrations, and the title
of the book. What do you think this book will be about?
While you are reading think about what may
happen next and why.

Monitor

As you read ask yourself if what you're reading makes sense.
If it doesn't, reread, look at the illustrations, or read ahead.

Question

Ask yourself questions about important ideas
in the story such as what the characters might
do or what you might learn.

Phonics

If there is a word that you do not know, look carefully
at the letters, sounds, and word parts that you do know.
Blend the sounds to read the word. Ask yourself if this is
a word you know. Does it make sense in the sentence?

Summarize

Think about the characters, the setting where the
story takes place, and the problem the characters faced
in the story. Tell the important ideas in the beginning,
middle, and end of the story.

Evaluate

Ask yourself questions like: Did you like the story?
Why or why not? How did the author make the story
come alive? How did the author make the story fun to
read? How well did you understand the story? Maybe
you can understand it better if you read it again!